To Jeff, Lilly, and Emma, my cent-sational family.
–K. W.

*For all my nieces and nephews
who hopefully are saving their pennies.*
–M. H.

Text copyright © 2022 Kimberly Wilson
Illustrations copyright © 2022 Mark Hoffmann

First published in 2022 by Page Street Kids
an imprint of
Page Street Publishing Co.
27 Congress Street, Suite 105
Salem, MA 01970
www.pagestreetpublishing.com

Distributed by Macmillan, sales in Canada by The Canadian Manda Group

22 23 24 25 26 CCO 5 4 3 2 1
ISBN-13: 978-1-64567-468-9
ISBN-10: 1-64567-468-1

CIP data for this book is available from the Library of Congress.

This book was typeset in Cabin.
The illustrations were done in acrylic, colored pencil, pan pastel, and digital.
Cover and book design by Julia Tyler for Page Street Kids

Printed and bound in Shenzhen, Guangdong, China

Page Street Publishing uses only materials from suppliers who are committed to
responsible and sustainable forest management.

Page Street Publishing protects our planet by donating to nonprofits like The Trustees,
which focuses on local land conservation.

trustees

A PENNY'S WORTH

KIMBERLY WILSON

illustrated by MARK HOFFMANN

PAGE
STREET
KiDS

STAMP!

Hot off the minting press, Penny sparkled.

"I FEEL LIKE A MILLION BUCKS!"

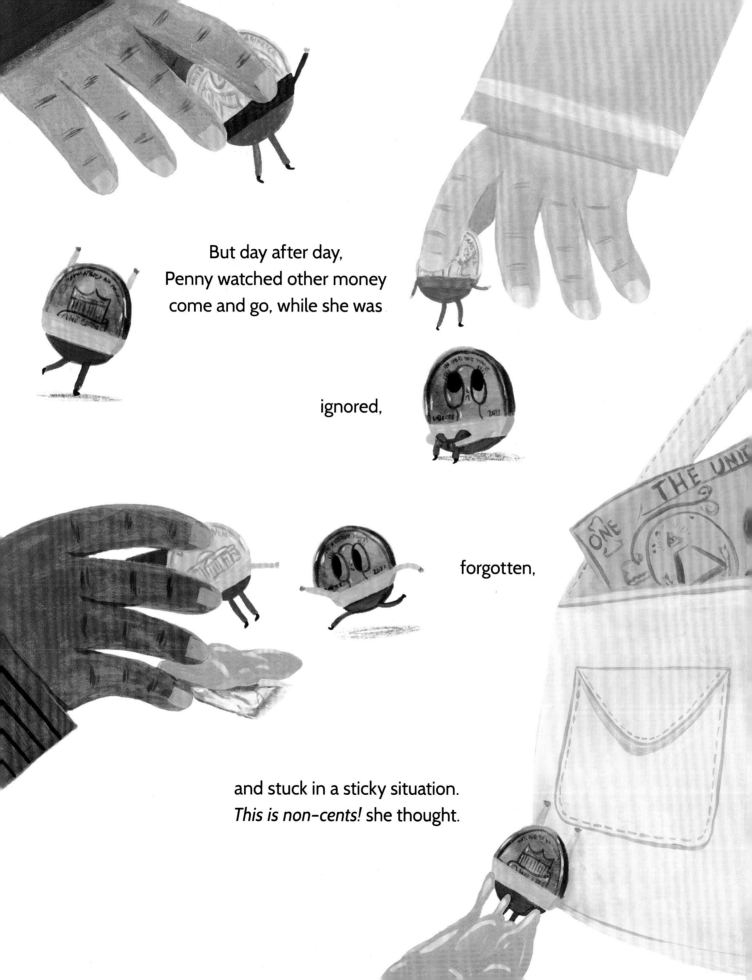

But day after day,
Penny watched other money
come and go, while she was

ignored,

forgotten,

and stuck in a sticky situation.
This is non-cents! she thought.

"HOWDY, BUCKAROO," Big Bill said.
"Why the long face?"

"I want in on the action too," Penny said.

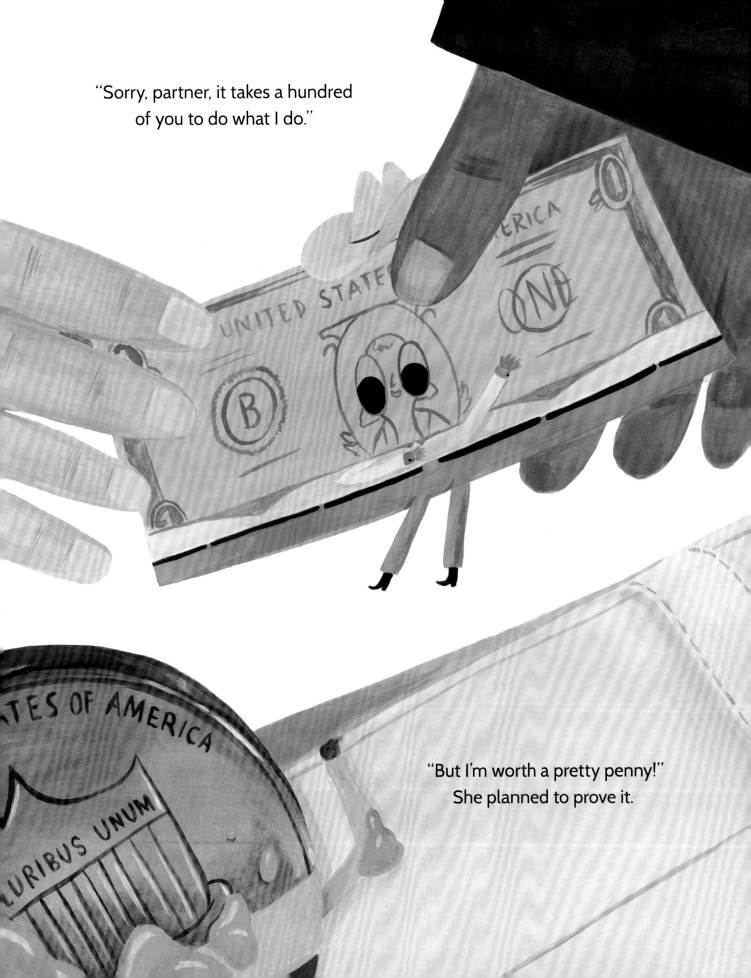

"Sorry, partner, it takes a hundred
of you to do what I do."

"But I'm worth a pretty penny!"
She planned to prove it.

"Arcade games!" Penny cheered.

"WHOA, COOL YOUR COPPER."
Quarter stopped her. "Slot surfin' is quarters-only. You're twenty-four cents short."

"What?! But I'm cent-sational!"

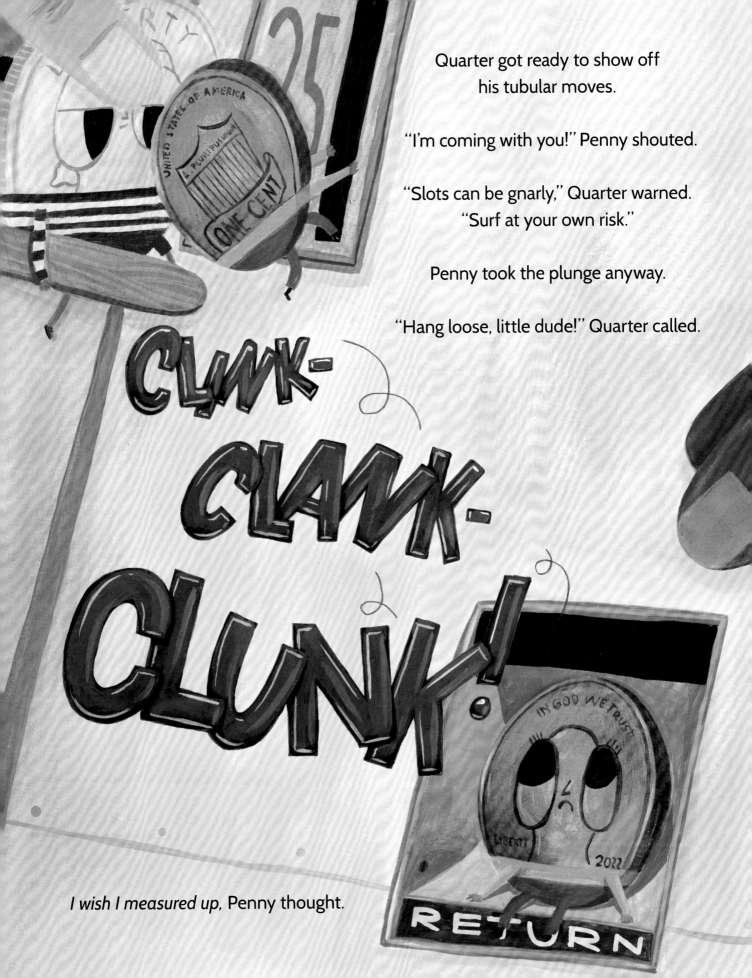

Quarter got ready to show off
his tubular moves.

"I'm coming with you!" Penny shouted.

"Slots can be gnarly," Quarter warned.
"Surf at your own risk."

Penny took the plunge anyway.

"Hang loose, little dude!" Quarter called.

CLINK-
CLANK-
CLUNK!

I wish I measured up, Penny thought.

RETURN

Penny kept a lookout for her next chance.
"Penny candy! I was made for this!"

"1–2–3, EYES ON ME." Dime drew a diagram.
"You need ten cents to be worth a dime."

"But it's penny candy!"

"Time for a quick history lesson," Dime said.
"Did you know pennies used to pay for
gobstoppers, lollipops, and even licorice sticks?"

"I knew it!" Penny rejoiced.

"But now, candy costs more."
Disappointment spread across Penny's face.
"Keep your head up, little one."

I wish I were worth more. Penny sniffled.

Penny wriggled free,
charged on,
and knocked into Nickel.

"Sorry! Didn't see you there."

"Nobody does anymore," Nickel sighed.

"But you're five!" Penny exclaimed.
"I bet together we could do something worthwhile!"

"That's only six cents," he grumbled.
"We don't add up to much."

"It's worth a try."

Nickel declined.

I wish I were enough on my own.
Penny slumped.

Then Penny saw the headline.

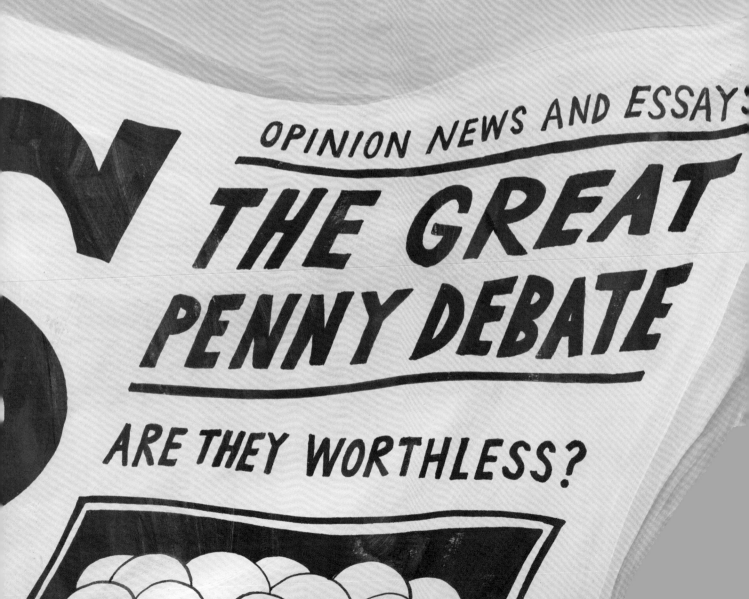

OPINION NEWS AND ESSAYS

THE GREAT PENNY DEBATE

ARE THEY WORTHLESS?

"I'm not worth ANYTHING?!"
This threw her in a tailspin and sent her over the edge.

Tattered and torn up,
Penny imagined life as a sewer cent.

Ignored.

Forgotten.

Stuck.

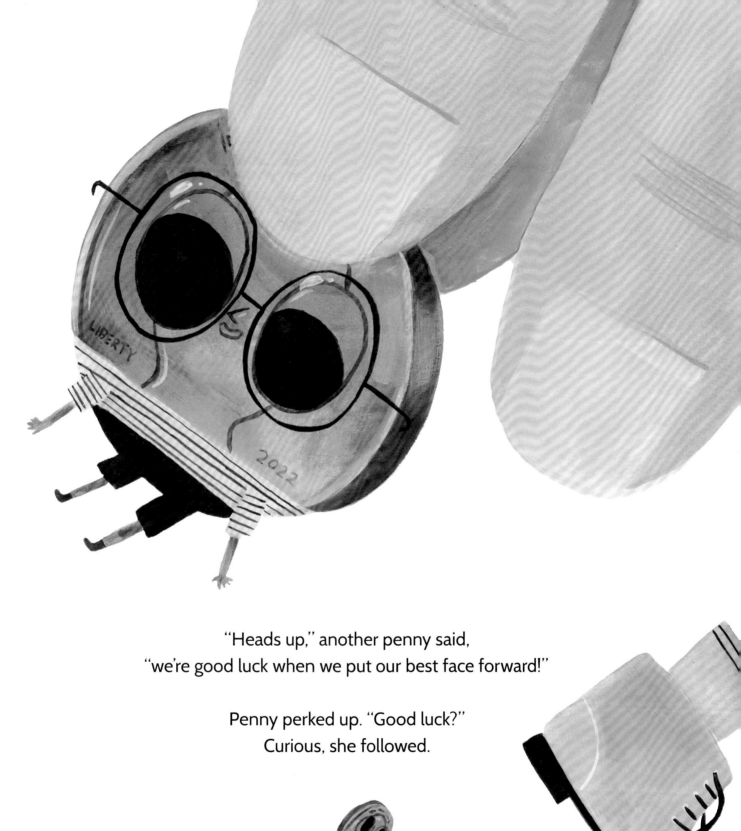

"Heads up," another penny said,
"we're good luck when we put our best face forward!"

Penny perked up. "Good luck?"
Curious, she followed.

Penny clung to a shoelace.
And when thrown for a loop,
she caught a wave.

"COWABUNGA, DUDE!"

Then she stopped . . .

dropped . . .

and rolled . . .

And there they were . . .
Pennies—glowing, flying, flipping!
Kids—searching, smiling, tossing!

Penny could not make heads or tails of it,
but something inside her changed.

With her best face forward,
Penny caught a child's eye.
This is my time to shine!
She listened to his whisper.

A WISH!
Penny knew how important wishes could be.

She beamed. *He can count on me!*

The child tossed Penny in the air.
Up-up-up she flew.
Leading with her heart, she dove headfirst—

The child smiled.

"Wishes do come true," Penny said.
"I'M PRICELESS!"

For the first time, everything made cents.

TWO CENTS' WORTH OF FUN FACTS

- It's only coin-cidence that National One Cent Day shares a date with April Fool's Day and is celebrated every April 1st. (No joke!) The holiday commemorates the first US one-cent coin produced in a private mint in 1787.

- In the early 1900s, a penny could pay for a game at the penny arcade or individually wrapped penny candy, like a Tootsie Roll®.

- Superstition says finding a penny lying face up is good luck, but if you find it face down, flip it over and leave it for the next person.

- The idea of wishing on pennies while throwing them into a well or fountain began in ancient times as an offering and prayer to the gods for clean water. Now many wishing coins tossed into fountains are donated to charities, making their value even more meaningful.

A HEADS UP ON PENNIES

Currently, pennies cost almost double their face value to produce. Because of this, there is a movement to stop production altogether. In fact, other countries like Canada have already stopped minting their pennies. Despite all of this, pennies remain the most minted coin in the United States, with five to ten billion produced each year.

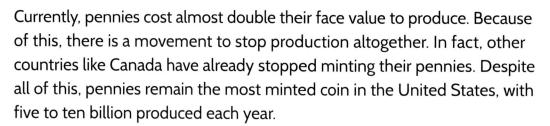

GET YOUR MONEY'S WORTH

1 DOLLAR

= 4 quarters, 10 dimes, 20 nickels, or 100 pennies

1 QUARTER

= 5 nickels or 25 pennies

1 DIME

= 2 nickels or 10 pennies

1 NICKEL

= 5 pennies

BIBLIOGRAPHY

U.S. Mint, www.usmint.gov

"Kids: U.S. Mint for Kids." Kids | U.S. Mint for Kids, www.usmint.gov/learn/kids

"NATIONAL ONE CENT DAY - April 1." National Day Calendar, 31 Mar. 2020, www.nationaldaycalendar.com/days-2/national-one-cent-day-april-1

"The History of Penny Candy." Le Cordon Bleu | The History of Penny Candy, www.chefs.edu/culinary-central/13/05/the-history-of-penny-candy

"Weird Money Facts: Why We Throw Money in Fountains." Wise Bread, www.wisebread.com/weird-money-facts-why-we-throw-money-in-fountains